THE THREE PIGS

DAVID WIESNER

Clarion Books • New York

To David Macaulay

&

To Carol Goldenberg

with gratitude

And special thanks to Andi Stern

Clarion Books
a Houghton Mifflin Company imprint
215 Park Avenue South
New York, NY 10003
Copyright © 2001 by David Wiesner

The artwork was executed in watercolor, gouache, colored inks,
pencil, and colored pencil on Fabriano hot press paper.
The text was set in 17.5-point New Century Schoolbook and
16-point Benguiat Book (and in manipulated forms of these faces),
18-point Tekton, and 42-point Dom Casual.
Art direction and typography by Carol Goldenberg.

Library of Congress Cataloging-in-Publication Data

Wiesner, David.
The three pigs / by David Wiesner.
p. cm.
Summary: The three pigs escape the wolf by going into another world where
they meet the cat and the fiddle, the cow that
jumped over the moon, and a dragon.
ISBN 0-618-00701-6
[1. Pigs—Fiction. 2. Characters in literature—Fiction.]
I. Three little pigs. English. II. Title.
PZ7.W6367 Th   2001
[E]—dc21   00-057016
LBM 10 9 8 7 6 5 4 3 2

Once upon a time there were three pigs who went out into the world to seek their fortune. The first pig decided to build a house, and he built it out of straw.

Along came a wolf, who knocked at the door and said, "Little pig, little pig, let me come in."

And the pig answered, "Not by the hair of my chinny-chin-chin." The wolf said, "Then I'll huff and I'll puff and I'll blow your house in!"

Now, the second pig built his house out of sticks. Along came the wolf, who knocked at the door and said, "Little pig, little pig, let me come in."

And the pig answered, "Not by the hair of my chinny-chin-chin." The wolf said, "Then I'll huff and I'll puff and I'll blow your house in!"

So the wolf huffed, and he puffed, and he blew the house in . . . and ate the pig up.

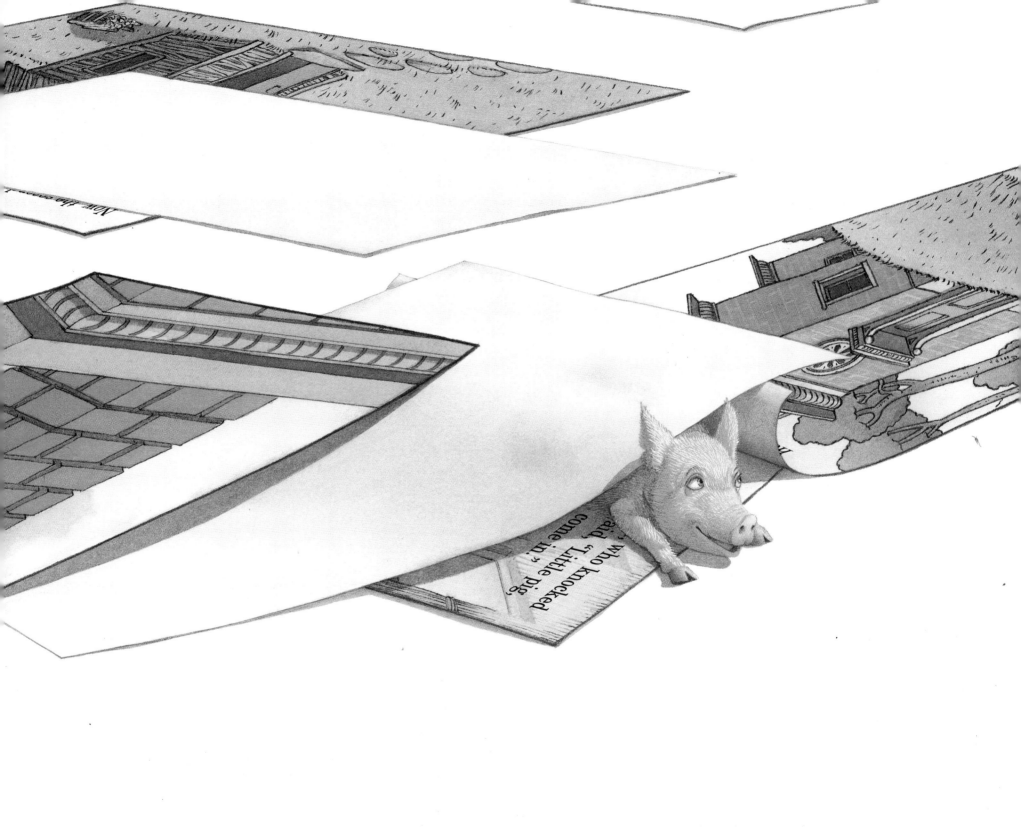

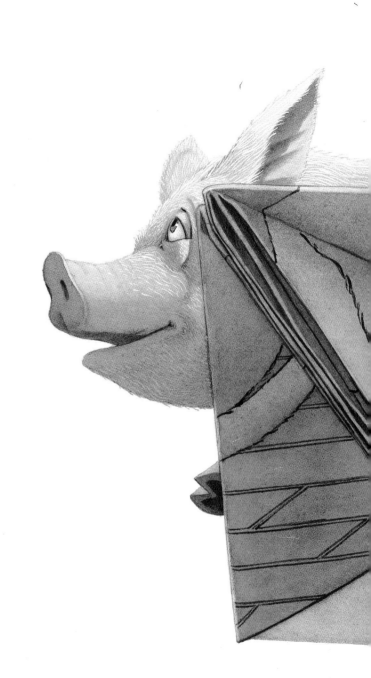

Hey
diddle diddle,
The cat and the fiddle,
The cow jumped
over the moon.

High on a hill there lived a great dragon, who stood guard over a rose made of the purest gold.

The prince spurred his steed to the mountaintop, drew his sword, and slew the mighty dragon.

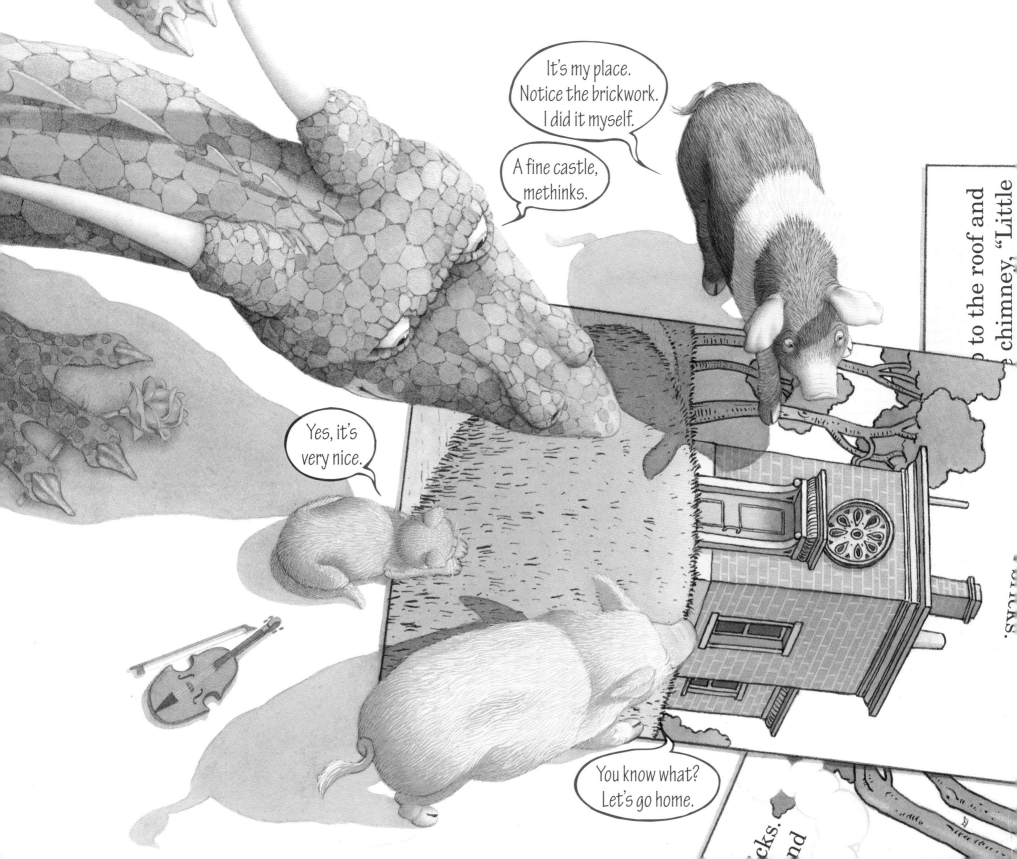

...hird pig built his ...ut of bricks.

Along came a wolf, who knocked at the door and said, "Little pig, little pig, let me come in."

And the pig answered, "Not by the hair of my chinny-chin-chin."

The wolf said, "Then I'll huff and I'll puff and I'll blow your house in!"

The wolf huffed, and he
But no matter how much he puffed, as
could not blow down th brick house